D0329029

The Ups and Downs
of Jorie Jenkins

BETTY BATES

The Ups and Downs
of Jorie Jenkins

HOLIDAY HOUSE · New York

MARCELLUS LIBRARY
Marcellus Community Schools

Copyright © 1978 by Betty Bates
All rights reserved
Printed in the United States of America

Library of Congress Cataloging in Publication Data'

Bates, Betty.
    The ups and downs of Jorie Jenkins.

    SUMMARY: A young girl must adjust to her father's
serious illness.
    [1. Family life—Fiction] I. Title.
PZ7.B2945Up   [Fic]   77–16698
ISBN 0–8234–0321–1

FOR TOM, DAN, LARRY, AND SALLY
WHO GENEROUSLY SHARED
THEIR UPS AND DOWNS WITH ME

Contents

The Ups and Downs
of Jorie Jenkins

1 • My Own Original Recipe

How come Craig Tanner always calls me Shrimp? I mean, he's twice as tall as I am, but wouldn't you think he'd have a little respect? After all, I'm the only girl who can make it under Mrs. Corrigan's fence and take the shortcut on the way to school. I get there dirty, but I get there fast.

Come to think of it, I won't be taking that shortcut any more. We're not in grade school this year. Tomorrow, we start junior high, and if creepy Craig Tanner turns out to be in my homeroom I'll walk out.

Still, it'll be fun seeing the kids from my old school again, the ones I haven't seen all summer, and besides I'll get to meet a lot of new kids. It's scary, but it's exciting.

Anyway, I don't have time now to think about junior high. My caramel syrup is boiling. See, Dad and Mom and I are putting my big sister Marcia on the plane for Arizona this afternoon, and I'm out in the kitchen cooking up something for her to take with her. It's my own original recipe that I just made up, and it's a combination of corn flakes and caramel syrup. I take this hot caramel syrup and——"Ouch! Ooh, ouch!"

Holy Sam! I spilled it on my bare foot. All of a sudden, I'm hopping around the kitchen doing this war dance with Sparks the Schnauzer yipping at my toes. Wowie, does it hurt!

The door from outside opens, and in walks Dad. "Hey, Jorie, what's all the yelling? I could hear you across the street."

"I burned my foot. Ooh, Dad, it hurts. What'll I dooo?"

"Take it easy, sweetheart." He grabs the mixing bowl and fills it with water and sticks it on the floor. "Get down on the floor." He helps me down and picks up my foot and carefully lets it down into the water. "There. Feel any better?"

"Yeah, it's better. It's so much better." I breathe out slowly. My foot's beginning to feel like a foot again.

See, my dad's a doctor. Actually he's a children's doctor. A pediatrician. That's how come he knows all about burns. All my life he's been rescuing me and Marcia when we get into these horrible fixes with scratches and bumps and broken bones and all that stuff. He can fix everything.

"Thanks, Dad," I say now. "You can fix everything."

"Come on, Jorie, I can't fix everything. I can't fix clogged pipes or broken joints or things that need mending. Except on kids, of course."

He's always saying these goofy things that ought to sound crazy, only they don't.

He kneels down and examines my foot in the water. "Looks okay. First-degree burn is all." When he stands up, his tennis shoes make this scrunching noise where some caramel syrup came off my foot onto the floor. Sparks is over by the stove licking up a puddle of the stuff and getting it all over his whiskers. Dad takes this big sniff. "Hey, you must be cooking up something spectacular."

"Caramel crispies. I'm making 'em for Marcia to take on the plane. It's my own original recipe. See, I take this hot caramel syrup and pour it over corn flakes and mix 'em up, and then I pour the whole mess in a pan and let it get hard and cut it in squares."

"So did you pour the caramel syrup with your foot?"

" 'Course not. I spilled half of it when I knocked over the pan on the stove, and it landed on my foot."

"Left the handle sticking out, huh?"

"Yeah. I know, I know. I forgot you're not supposed to do that."

"So make half as many caramel crispies. They sound terrific." He dropped the subject of the sticking-out handle. That's one thing that's so great about him. He doesn't give these boring lectures about what you're not supposed to do.

He picks up his tennis racket. He's been playing tennis with Dr. Finch. I can't figure out how come he plays with Dr. Finch. I can't stand Dr. Finch. He's always patting my cheek and calling me Carrots on account of my red hair. I mean, Carrots! But today's Labor Day, and Dad plays with him on Sunday and holiday afternoons if they can get away after they do their hospital rounds. Dad's this health nut. Six feet three, and he weighs two twenty. "I'm as healthy as a bear," he always says, patting his waistline. Talk about goofy things.

Lately, he hasn't been playing much, though. Seems as if it gets harder and harder for him to get away, and his waistline is getting baggier and baggier. He doesn't pat it much any more.

"You've got a bunch of messages on the hall table, Dad. Mrs. Jasper's just about hysterical 'cause her new baby threw up half his formula."

"Okay, I'll call her before I take my shower. Where's your mom?"

"She's up helping Marcia try and close her suitcase."

He reaches down and sticks his finger against the end of my nose. Gently, just to show he likes me. I like it when he does that. Out in the hall, he picks up the messages and dashes upstairs singing, "I've been working on the railroad, all the livelong day. I've been working on the railroad, and now I'm old and gray." He never remembers words, so he makes up his own.

I yank my foot out of the water. It still hurts, but I guess I'm going to live. I stand on one foot and pour the water out of the mixing bowl and measure in two cups of corn flakes. I pour the hot sauce over them and stir.

I hope Marcia likes my crispies. I think she's the tiniest bit scared about going all the way out to Arizona, even though she is five years older than me. She's going to visit Dad's mother for almost a week, before high school begins, and Gran's going to drive her all around out west looking at colleges for next year. Gran's really neat. She always comes for Thanksgiving and Christmas, and she always acts as if she's been waiting all year just to see us. She brings these sweaters and stuff she makes for us, and everything always fits right. How does she know?

"Whatcha making, Jorie?"

There's Marcia standing in the kitchen doorway in her pink robe with the blue print blouse over her arm that she hemmed just this morning. She's watching me with those enormous blue eyes of hers. Wonder how long she's been there. The caramel crispies are supposed to be a last-minute surprise.

"Oh—um—just messing around. You get the suitcase closed?"

She giggles so her dimples show. "Just barely. I had to sit on it while Mom fastened it. Hope it doesn't bust open on the plane." She opens the door to the basement and clumps downstairs to press the blouse.

Funny. I've got this weird feeling. I mean, I hardly know it's there, but there it is. I'm the tiniest bit glad she's going away. Now it's for only a week, but next year it'll be for the whole school year. See, she sort of takes after Dad. She's not big or anything, even though she does have to watch her weight. But she's got his blue eyes, and hair the color of applesauce, and dimples in both cheeks. She's got his nose too. A strong nose, Dad calls it. But Marcia's always complaining about hers. When she finished her junior year in high school in June, Mom asked her if she wanted her nose bobbed, and she got all indignant and said she'd never do an artificial thing like that. Well, does she want that nose or doesn't she?

Anyway, there's this thing between her and Dad. I've got this sneaking idea that he feels kind of special about her. Maybe because she's pretty and quiet and shy sometimes. Or maybe because she looks like him. Of course, I think he feels special about me too. Maybe because I'm not quiet, and I'm little and redheaded like Mom. But it's two different kinds of special. Anyway, I've got this sort of relieved feeling, because with Marcia gone next year I'll have Dad to myself. Except for Mom, of course. Maybe it's awful to feel that way, but I guess you can't help how you feel.

I shove one of the crispies into my mouth. Ooh boy! It's all I can do to chew it. It sticks to my teeth so I think I'll never get them apart, and I have to scrunch around inside my mouth with my finger and dig the blobs out. But it doesn't taste too bad. The rest of the crispies I line up inside a box.

I yank my tennis shoes out from under the breakfast table and start putting them on so I'll be ready to go out to the airport. It hurts when I stick my burned foot into the shoe, but I close my eyes and push.

"Jorie, you're not planning to wear those smelly shoes to the airport." It's Mom, standing in the middle of the kitchen floor giving me the once-over.

"C'mon, Mom, they don't smell." I grab the other shoe and jab it under my nose and breathe in hard. It smells.

I must be making a face because Mom says, "See, Jorie? Now you go up and put your clogs on."

Sometimes she makes me sick. How come she's making such a big thing about my dumb old clogs? "But, Mom, my clogs are all sticky from the root beer Stephanie and I made yesterday. It exploded out of the bottle." Stephanie's my best friend. Tomorrow, she and I are going to junior high together. Lots of times we do crazy things, and Mom likes some of them more than others.

Mom gives this big sigh. "Jorie, why didn't you wear your tennis shoes yesterday?"

"Listen, how was I supposed to know the stuff was gonna bust out like that? We followed the recipe just the way——"

"Then go and wipe the root beer off your clogs. And remember to wear them to school tomorrow too. Put your tennis shoes in the laundry." She starts over toward the food cupboard, and she must have stepped in one of the sticky spots because she stops and wrinkles up her nose.

"I'm gonna clean it up, Mom. Don't worry, I'll clean it up."

She gets out this rag and wipes off her shoe. She opens the cupboard. "I thought Marcia might like a bag of cookies to munch on the plane."

"But, Mom, I made her something. Caramel crispies."

"Why, Jorie, that's—um—very thoughtful of you."

How come she doesn't look too happy? Sure, I left the sugar out of the meringues that one time, but that was a whole month ago. Sometimes I don't think she's got any faith in me.

Marcia comes downstairs into the hall, and Dad brings the suitcase. "Where's Sparks? I've got to walk him before we leave." He walks Sparks every chance he gets, whenever he's not checking babies at the hospital, or whenever he's not at the office or at some medical meeting. Or whenever he hasn't had to rush off to examine some kid that fell out of a tree. Sometimes, I think he's kind of a superman. Seems as if everybody else thinks so too because the phone's always ringing when he's home.

The phone rings now. It's the hospital calling Dad. "One of the newborns?" he says into the phone. "Mmm. Better check it out. I'll be over."

"Oh, Dad!" Marcia's voice is a wail. "Can't they get somebody else?"

"There isn't anybody else. You know Bill Moy's gone for the weekend. Mom can drive you to the airport. Would somebody walk Sparks for me?" He wraps Marcia up in his big arms and holds her tight for what seems like ages. "Listen, sweetheart, you watch out for those cowboys out there." Then, very fast, he lets go. He pushes the end of my nose to say good-bye, and gives Mom this quick kiss. On his way out he snitches a caramel crispy out of the box.

I hope his teeth don't stick together.

Marcia just stands there. "Oh, Mom, how could he just go off like that?"

Mom puts her hand on Marcia's arm. "I'm sorry."

She always says that. Is that all she can say? Just "I'm sorry"? She opens the hall closet and gets out Marcia's coat. "Marcia, did you pack the glasses case you made for Gran?"

"Oh, no, I forgot. And I haven't got any place to pack it."

"Stuff it in your coat pocket. But hurry. It's almost four-thirty. I'll walk Sparks. Change your shoes, Jorie, and wipe up those spots in the kitchen."

How come she has to go and say that? She knows I'm planning to wipe up those spots.

I grab the box of caramel crispies and go upstairs. I find Marcia in her room looking for Gran's gift. I hand her my box. "Maybe you can stuff this in your other pocket. It's my own original recipe. They're kind of sticky, but you can pull 'em off your teeth with your finger."

"Oh, Jorie!" All of a sudden she gives me this

big hug, and I find myself hugging her back. For some crazy reason, I think of the time she let me use her makeup when I was only six and getting ready to be a bee in my ballet recital.

Sure, I'm glad Marcia's going away next year, but I'm going to miss her. I mean, with her gone who's going to help me spell symmetrical and unstick my stuck zippers?

I turn and hurry into my room to wipe off my clogs.

I'm back in the kitchen cleaning up the spots when Mom comes back in with Sparks. The phone rings, and she hurries to answer. "Hello. Yes, this is Mrs. Jenkins. He—he what? But he was just——" She stands there listening. "Of course," she says, "I'll be right over." She hangs up and closes her eyes. Her face is white.

"Mom! You okay?"

She opens her eyes and takes this deep breath. "That was one of the nurses at the hospital, Jorie. Dad collapsed in the elevator. Dr. Finch thinks it's a heart attack."

2 • Junior High

Over at the hospital, the Cardiac Care unit is like some weird nightmare. The beds are in these icky little cubicles around the edge of the room. There's this machine at the head of Dad's bed that looks like a TV, with squiggly lines going across it, like something out of some space movie. I hardly recognize him. He's got things going up his nostrils and tubes hanging down from over the bed and hooked up all over him. He looks— well, he looks like some ghost. His eyes are all droopy, and his face is powder white. He's not smiling or anything. He's just blank, as if he'd flopped down and forgotten all about us. How could he do that? How could he just forget about us?

I guess it's not his fault, but it makes me mad. I wish I hadn't come.

There's this nurse with a round face who's got to be at least fifty. She and Marcia and I stand on one side of the bed while Mom leans over Dad. "Charlie," says Mom in this low voice. His eyelids flicker, and he moves his hand the least bit. That big hand that took care of my foot a while ago. Mom picks it up and squeezes it. She can hardly get close to him on account of the tubes, but she gives a little smile. "We're here, Charlie."

He seems to be trying to smile, but he can't. My dad can't smile. How come?

At the door on the way out, Marcia turns to the nurse. "Is he——Will he get better?"

What a dumb question! Naturally, he'll get better.

The nurse pats Marcia's arm and says in this soft voice, "Honey, we hope so. We all hope so. You know we think the world of your dad."

Funny. I never saw her before, but she thinks the world of my dad.

Out by the elevators, we meet Dr. Finch. He looks different in his white coat. More important. He gives Mom this big hug. The top of her head comes just under his mustache. "Janet, I'm sorry," he says.

"Oh, Dave, he looks awful!" I never heard her say anything like that before. And her voice is wobbly, like somebody else's voice.

Dr. Finch lets go of her. "Give him time, Janet. It's a coronary all right, but a big healthy guy like Charlie ought to come through in pretty good shape." He puts an arm around Marcia and the other around me. I can't help squirming.

"I'm not going away," says Marcia. "I'm staying home."

Mom looks her in the eye. "You're going, Marcia. You have to see about college."

"But, Mom——"

"Look, Marcia, we don't want to worry Gran any more than we have to." Her voice isn't quite so wobbly now. "If Dad should—should get worse, we'll let you and Gran know, and you can both come right away."

"How about leaving day after tomorrow?" says Dr. Finch. "By that time he should be much better, and after that your mother and Carrots can take care of things."

Carrots! I can't stand being called that. I can't stand Dr. Finch and his mustache and his scratchy white coat. It's partly his fault Dad had the heart attack in the first place. It's all on account of playing tennis with him.

I guess my mind isn't making any sense. I guess I'm mad at everybody.

Mom tells me I've got to go to school tomorrow, and she and Dr. Finch arrange for Mrs. Finch to call Gran, and to drive Marcia to the airport day after tomorrow. Meanwhile, we get to see Dad one more time after dinner for a few minutes, so we have to eat in the hospital cafeteria.

The cafeteria has these gloomy brown walls. I mean, brown walls! And snaky-looking plastic plants in one corner. We go through the line like a bunch of robots. Mom eats hardly anything. In fact nobody eats much, including me. I sit there staring at some corn pudding that looks like wet sand, and thinking. "How come they had to put those things up Dad's nose, Mom?"

"Those tubes? That's the oxygen. They've got to get oxygen into him."

"Yeah, I s'pose so."

There's this long silence. All of a sudden I remember Stephanie. "You got any money, Mom? I gotta go call Stephanie." I sound a hundred years old. I'm this hundred-year-old robot.

I take the money to the pay phone out in the hall. "I can't come over tonight," I tell Stephanie in my hundred-year-old voice.

"Who is this?"

"It's me. Jorie."

"Oh. You sound funny. Anyway, you gotta come over. It's our last night before junior high. Jorie, you said you'd come."

"Well, see, my dad's——He's—um—he's in the hospital."

"Sure. Your dad's always in the hospital."

"I mean he's sick. He's sick in the hospital."

"What's the matter with him? How come he's sick?"

The way she says that word sick, it's as if she thinks it's all his fault. "Look, Steph, he can't help it, I guess. See, it just happened. He—he had a heart attack." I can hardly say it. I guess the whole trouble is that I think it's all his fault too. I'm ashamed that my dad is sick.

"No wonder you sound funny. I'm sorry. Honest."

"Thanks, Steph."

"I guess you won't be going to school tomorrow."

"I gotta. Mom's making me go. I'll come by around ten of eight, the way we said. Okay?"

"Listen, my mom said she could drop us off on the way to work. She's gotta be at the shop early tomorrow."

I don't want to get driven by Stephanie's mom.

She's always asking questions. "Nah, let's walk. I'd rather walk."

"Well, okay. See you."

Stephanie's mom owns this stationery store downtown, and I guess I feel sort of inferior sometimes because Mom doesn't own a stationery store or sell real estate or run her own airline to Alaska. All Mom does is stuff like working at the hospital gift shop one day a week, or playing the piano for the Youth Center show, or planting tulip bulbs in front of the library. Stuff that doesn't seem very important.

When we get home that night and go to bed, the house seems awfully quiet. I lie there waiting for Dad to come in and remembering he's not going to. I think of Mom in her bedroom by herself, and Marcia in hers, and me in mine. I'll bet we're all lying awake waiting for Dad to come, and then remembering he won't.

The next morning after Mom and Marcia leave for the hospital, I leave for Stephanie's. Snakes are crawling around inside my stomach. How am I ever going to go to a brand-new school and face all those kids I never saw before? I got assigned this homeroom teacher by the name of Mr. Stern. He's probably some creaky old man with false teeth. Yesterday, I was all set for school, but now I don't want to go. All I want is to stay home and be miserable.

At school, Stephanie and I have to separate because we've been assigned to different rooms. In the hall outside my room the kids are all milling around talking and giggling. How can they be talking and giggling at a time like this?

Gretchen Bowlenberg's there, and Mike O'-Neil, from sixth grade at my old school. Naturally, I feel too rotten to talk to them. I don't feel the least bit like giggling, so I look the other way.

Ooh boy! There's somebody coming down the hall on crutches. It's Craig Tanner. He's going to be in my room. I'm walking out. I really am actually going to quit school right now. Only I can't. Mom would skin me alive. Besides, I can't do that to her. She's got enough problems.

"Hey, Jorie, how are you?" says Craig. What do you know? He didn't call me Shrimp. And how about those crutches and that big cast on his foot? He must have been in some accident. Well, who cares?

I look at the floor. "I'm okay." That's all that comes out. How come he's got to be so cheerful? Can't he see I feel rotten?

He gives me this puzzled look. "Boy-oh-boy, what's bugging you? You act as if I've got chicken pox or something. Aren't you even gonna ask what happened to my foot?"

I shrug. "So what happened to your foot? You musta got it caught in some rat trap."

"Hey, what's wrong with you anyway? It's bad enough I can't go out for football, and now you gotta make cracks about it. Why should I tell you about my foot if you're gonna be like that? Forget it." He hobbles over and starts talking to Mike O'Neil.

I don't care hardly at all. In fact, I'm glad he can't go out for football. He's always been obnoxious about being good at sports. He thinks he's so great because he can hit a baseball farther and run faster than anybody else. What's so great about that? Anyway, I'd never be able to explain why I didn't ask about his stupid old foot. I couldn't tell him about Dad. Was I supposed to say Dad's lying in the hospital all white and blah, with tubes going into him so you can hardly even get near him? Was I supposed to say Mom made me come to school even though my stomach's got snakes crawling around inside it?

Gretchen Bowlenberg comes up to me. "Hi,

Jorie." She smiles that icky smile of hers, with her whole mouthful of crooked teeth showing. How come I had to go and get assigned to the same homeroom as Gretchen? This is too much.

I hunch my shoulders and back up against the lockers along the wall. "Hello, Gretchen."

"How was your summer?"

"Okay."

Mom tells me to always be friendly to everybody. She says it never costs you anything. But how can I be friendly at a time like this, especially to Gretchen? So I don't even ask her how her summer went. I just stand there staring at the floor.

The door of the classroom opens, and a man comes out. He must be Mr. Stern. He's this short, bony guy who looks about thirty, maybe. At least he's not a creaky type, and his teeth look real. "All right," he says, running his fingers through his blob of hair. "Everybody inside. Last one in gets the seat in front of me."

Very funny.

All around the edges of the room are tanks with plants and weird little animals and fish inside them. Mr. Stern has got to be a science teacher. I want to get as far away from him as I can, so I flop

down in the seat at the back of the first row behind this tubby girl in a red blouse. Mr. Stern
starts calling roll while I stare into this tank with
fish swimming around inside it. There's this tube
going down into the tank. Makes me think about
Dad again. Everything reminds me of Dad.

After a while, I hear somebody saying in this
loud voice, "She's back there, Mr. Stern." It's
Craig. He's got this puzzled look on his face, with
his eyebrows all screwed into funny lines.

Mr. Stern stares at me. The whole class turns
and stares. There's this terrible silence. "Are you
Jorie Jenkins?" says Mr. Stern.

I nod.

He runs his fingers through the blob again. It's
the color of mud. "So you can hear me after all,
Jorie. I called your name three times. Why didn't
you answer?"

"I didn't hear you."

Somebody giggles.

Mr. Stern shakes his head. "How do you do it,
Jorie? You seem to be able to turn your ears off
and on in some mysterious way. One minute you
can't hear, and the next minute you can. Amazing. Maybe you'd better come and sit at the front
of the row. Maybe this handsome young man in

the front seat will trade with you." The handsome young man who's supposed to trade with me is Mike O'Neil, who's short with big ears. When I scuff past him on the way to the front seat, he scrunches his eyebrows and shrugs in this puzzled way. Everybody's watching me. The snakes are whizzing around my stomach.

How come I had to go and get a wise guy for a teacher?

Anyway, he doesn't bother me any more. He just stands up in front and asks for volunteers to help him take care of the plants and animals. A whole bunch of people raise their hands, including Mike, but I keep mine down. I'm not going to get stuck feeding some slithery snake. Mr. Stern talks and talks about how we're going to study animals and their environment. He passes out the science books and gives us this horrible assignment for tomorrow. We're supposed to study the whole first chapter. "It's about our own environment. After all, we're animals too."

Somebody behind me quacks like a duck. Some people giggle. Mr. Stern raises his eyebrows. "I see we have some barnyard life in the room," he says. Everybody shuts up.

In the first chapter there's this picture of a

dump heap, to show us the stuff that gets wasted. That's what I feel like. A dump heap.

English is in Mrs. Gordon's room. She's got this wide smile that lights up her face, which I'm not exactly in the mood for. And she's got this—um—this really full figure that the guys all make cracks about in whispers, which I don't happen to think is funny. Nothing's funny.

I make sure I answer when she calls roll, but most of the time I'm in this sort of trance. "For Thursday," she says at the end of the period, "I want you to do a theme on your hobby. That way we'll get to know more about each other."

In the hall on the way to math, everybody's talking about all the homework we're getting. Everybody except me. They all ignore me, including Gretchen, who's making friends with the girl in the red blouse.

In the cafeteria at lunch, Gretchen sits with the girl in the red blouse, and when I get through the food line their table is full. I look around for Stephanie, but she's nowhere. I guess she must eat lunch at a different time. The whole rest of the room seems to be full of scary-looking strangers. Well, I don't care. I take my tray to a table where there's this skinny girl at one end and this short, fat guy at the other end. I sit in the middle, and we all eat without saying anything. I guess if all I want to do is sit and be miserable, I ought to be happy. So how come I'm so miserable?

All afternoon I'm still in a trance. In music class and French class, and while we're on the way back to our lockers to pick up our science books. Maybe I won't do that science assignment. Maybe I'll skip school tomorrow. The way I feel I'll never come back to this dump. While I'm getting the book out of my locker, Craig and Mike come by on their way out.

"Hi, Shrimp," says Craig. I turn around and stick my tongue out at him.

I hope he breaks his other foot.

Out in the playground I spot this tall, blond girl who turns out to be Stephanie. Boy-oh-boy, am I glad to see her! "Hey, Jorie," she says, "how'd you get along?"

"Awful. It was just awful. Craig Tanner got mad at me, and Mr. Stern made fun of me, and everybody else just ignored me."

"That's terrible. That's just plain mean after what happened to your dad."

"How would they know what happened to my dad?"

"Y'mean, you didn't tell 'em?"

"Nope. It's none of their business."

"Oh, Jorie, that's dumb. You're just plain dumb."

Well, that makes it unanimous. Now everybody in the whole school is mad at me.

3 • My Favorite and Unfavorite Places

"Steph, do I look sick?"

" 'Course not. Why would you look sick?"

"I feel awful. My head feels as if it's on fire. And I feel dizzy. I think I'm gonna faint."

"That's silly. Honestly, Jorie, I just don't understand what's the matter with you. I mean, I'm sorry about your dad, and you're my best friend, and I really do want to help. But you're acting strange. Really strange."

We're on our way home from school now, and I can't see why she can't be more sympathetic. That's the absolute truth about my head feeling fiery. I think I'm going to pass out on the sidewalk. It's scary.

When we get to Stephanie's house, she says, "Wanna come in? I learned this new piece for my piano lesson. It's a Chopin waltz."

"Nah."

"Oh, c'mon, Jorie. I need you to tell me if I've got the rhythm right. Chopin's tricky, y'know."

"Well, I hope you and Chopin will be very happy together, but I gotta get home."

I leave her standing there staring. I know what she's thinking. She's thinking I ought to quit acting weird. But I can't help it. I want the whole world to break down and cry for me. Can't they see?

When I get home, the lawn service truck is just driving away. Sparks meets me at the door, but he doesn't jump all over me the way he used to. He's been awfully quiet lately. He must miss Dad. Mom and Marcia aren't home. They're at the hospital with Dad, of course. The house seems dead without Mom, spooky even. I get this feeling I'm the only person in the world, that nobody else is alive. Thank goodness I'm meeting Mom and Marcia at the hospital for dinner.

I get out milk and graham crackers. The phone rings. It's one of Mom's friends in the garden club. "I just heard the news, Jorie. Is there anything I can do?" What can she do? Wave some kind of a magic wand that'll make Dad well again? I wish she and the whole garden club would take their flower pots and stick them over their heads.

"Thanks, but there's really nothing you can do."

"Well, please tell your mother I called."

Right after I hang up the phone rings again. It's Mrs. Spinner. Her husband directs the junior-senior show, and she's the choreographer. "Oh, Jorie, I'm so sorry. Is there anything we can do?"

I wish people would quit saying that. "There's nothing, Mrs. Spinner."

There's this long pause. Finally she says, "Jorie, do you think your mother will be able to play the piano for the show this year? I hate to bother you about it, but I've got to start getting a committee together. Tryouts are less than a month away."

How can she think about tryouts at a time like this?

"I don't think Mom can do it, Mrs. Spinner. She's spending all her time at the hospital. I think you'd better get somebody else."

"Well, all right, we'll dig up somebody. Is Marcia going to try out this year?"

"I don't know, Mrs. Spinner." Marcia tried out

last year, and she ended up in the chorus. There must have been a thousand girls in that chorus.

"Well, tell your mother we're all thinking about her and your dad. We'll send flowers when he gets better."

Yeah. When he gets better.

I wish people wouldn't call. Funny. A while ago I wanted the whole world to break down and cry for me, and now I wish people would leave me alone. I'm all mixed up.

I grab the milk and crackers and hurry out in back with Sparks. The phone rings in the house, but I ignore it. Dad's answering service can take the message. Maybe they can think of something the person can do.

Way out past Mom's vegetable garden, by the back fence, there's this crab apple tree. When I sit out there, I just fit under the branches. Of course, I've got to be careful not to squish any apples when I sit down. But it's like being in some special little room. It's my favorite place. I can be alone there and think, or else I can be alone and not think.

Only not now. There's the sound of a power mower, and it's coming closer and closer. It's in Mr. Kirby's yard behind ours, on the other side of the fence. There's this guy pushing the mower.

I've seen him around all summer taking care of Mr. Kirby's yard, ever since Mr. Kirby broke his hip in June. This guy is eighteen or nineteen maybe. Dark and skinny, with big shoulders. He comes up to the fence, and he stops and turns off the mower and wipes the sweat off his forehead with his arm. Sparks is up by the fence now, barking like mad. The guy stoops and pats Sparks on the nose and talks to him in this low voice, and Sparks quits barking. All of a sudden, the guy sees me squinting at him from under the tree, and he gives me this very surprised look, as if maybe he's seeing a ghost.

"Hi," I say. What are you supposed to say when somebody thinks you're a ghost?

He smiles this very shy smile. "Hi," he says.

"How's Mr. Kirby?"

"Lots better. He gets around okay with a cane now." There's something different about the way the guy talks. He's got this teeny accent. Maybe he came from somewhere, like Spain or South America or Acapulco.

"I'm glad he's better," I say.

I figure the conversation is over, but he stands up and leans on the fence and says, "How's Marcia?"

I scrunch over to where I can see his face from

under the branches. "Marcia? Y'mean my sister Marcia?"

He nods.

"How come you know my sister Marcia?"

"When I was in high school I knew her." He looks down at the grass. "She wouldn't remember me, though."

"Sure she would. What's your name?"

"Peter. Peter Diaz."

"Peter who?"

"Diaz. D-I-A-Z. Rhymes with *he has*. Marcia and I had the same adviser, that's all."

"How come you know she lives here?"

His face turns red. "I—I just happened to see her once. She was going in the front door."

"Hey, do you like my sister?"

His face gets redder. His hands are rolled into fists on top of the fence. All of a sudden, he looks me in the eye. "Is that your business?"

"You're mad, aren't you? Hey, I didn't mean to make you mad." I gulp down a swallow of milk. "Marcia's going away tomorrow."

"Y'mean, she——She's not leaving town, is she? She'll be back, won't she?"

He likes my sister.

I nod. "She'll be back Sunday. She's just visiting Grandma. She's looking at colleges for next year. You going to college?"

It turns out he's just started at the junior college on the west side of town, near where he lives on Seventeenth Street. He's been earning money for a couple of years working at one of the supermarkets, and all summer he's been doing Mr. Kirby's yard work too, ever since he graduated from high school in June.

"You gonna keep on working for Mr. Kirby even though he's better?"

"Sure. He still needs me, and I need the money. And besides——" He swallows and looks away. Now I'm positive he likes Marcia. He's hoping he can get to know her. Funny. Marcia's never had a real boyfriend. She seems to be scared of boys, as if they're lions escaped from some zoo.

"Hey, where'd you get that accent?"

He gives me that look again. "What accent?"

"You've got this teeny accent. As if you came from somewhere else. Where'd you get it?"

"You don't mind asking personal questions, do you?"

"That's not personal. Anyway, I like your accent. I didn't say there was anything wrong with it. How come you're so touchy?"

"I'm not touchy. Anyway, I came from Cuba."

"Hey, you're a Cuban refugee."

"If that's what you call it. I gotta get back to work or Mr. Kirby'll fire me." He turns toward the mower, but then he looks back over his shoulder and gives me that smile of his, and this wink. "Thanks for the information."

He starts up the mower and pushes away on his long legs.

I wanted to ask him a million more questions. I mean, it's not every day you meet a refugee. Peter. Peter Diaz that rhymes with *he has*. I've got to ask Marcia if she remembers him. I'll bet she does.

How did he get out of Cuba? Maybe he smuggled himself out in a plane. Where's his family? Maybe he's an orphan. Maybe they killed his dad and mom. Then how come they didn't kill him? How come he won't stick around and answer my questions? Am I too nosy? Dad always says I'm too nosy. Wait till I tell him about Peter.

Only I can't tell him. Not now.

At dinner in the cafeteria, Mom says, "Dad's better today, Jorie. Dave Finch arranged for you to see him tonight, even though they don't usually allow routine visits from twelve-year-olds. He thinks it would do Dad good."

"Oh, Mom, do I have to?"

She looks puzzled. "Well, if you'd rather
not——"

"No, I'll go. I want to. I really do."

I don't want to go, but still I'm going. I've got
to. I must be crazy.

Marcia's pretty tired. She leaves right after dinner so she can go home and get ready to go away
all over again. "Get to bed early," says Mom.
"You've got to get some sleep."

In the Cardiac Care unit it's spooky quiet. All
I can hear is the breathing of the patients. There's
a nurse there with stringy blond hair, sitting at
this place in the middle of the room where they've
got a whole bunch of these machines with squiggly lines. She gives Mom this very faint smile.
Mom looks tired. I never saw her look tired before. Or maybe I never noticed.

I feel shivery. It must be cold in here. Or else
I just feel cold with all the machines around me,
and the icky white lights and the white sheets on
the metal beds, and all the people lying there and
not saying anything and just breathing.

Dad's eyes are closed. He looks as if he's never
going to get up, as if he's going to stay flopped
down under those white sheets forever. I edge in
next to Mom. How can she stand to be here? I

hate it. I hate seeing sick people and metal beds and plastic bags and tubes hanging down. I don't know what to do. Am I supposed to say something to Dad? Mom takes his hand. "Jorie's here, Charlie. See? It's Jorie, Charlie."

His eyelids flicker and open. I lean over as far as I can without bumping the tubes. I want him to see me. "Hi, Dad."

"Hi, sweetheart." I think he's trying to smile. All of a sudden he closes one eye and then opens it.

He winked at me. Sure he did. First Peter did, and now Dad.

My eyes go blurry. This big sob takes hold of me and shakes me. All of a sudden, I'm crying as though I'm never going to stop, and Mom puts her arms around me and holds me close.

4 • I Don't Wanna Talk About It

Nobody actually says anything, but somehow I get this feeling Dad isn't doing so well. I don't like thinking about it. Mom stayed at the hospital all day yesterday and the day before, visiting him as often as they let her, and when she came home at night she didn't say much, maybe because there wasn't much to say.

I'm getting my own breakfasts now because she goes to the hospital early. She used to make oatmeal a lot, and I like it even though I guess people my age aren't supposed to. But I don't feel like making it for myself. This morning, I drink orange juice out of the can. It's too much trouble to mix it with water. It tastes awful, but it's easier that way. And shredded wheat with piles of sugar and milk.

It's no fun eating by myself. It's lonesome. Thank goodness Marcia's coming home on Sunday, day after tomorrow. She can even cook a little, so I won't get stuck with canned hash all the time. The only things I like to cook are candies and stuff like that.

At school today it turns out my class has gym with Stephanie's class. Boy, are we glad to see each other! While we're in line to get our locker assignments, while everybody else is talking and giggling about the boys in their rooms, Stephanie says to me, "Did you ever tell Mr. Stern about your dad?"

Gretchen Bowlenberg's voice, behind us, says, "Tell him what, Stephanie? What's the matter with Jorie's dad?"

"If you've really gotta know," says Stephanie, "he had this heart attack."

Gretchen gasps. "A heart attack. Jorie, I'm terribly, terribly sorry. How come you didn't say so? How come you didn't tell Mr. Stern?"

How come she doesn't shut up?

At lunch, Gretchen grabs my arm and leads me over to her table. We haven't even sat down before she blabs about my dad. There's this awful silence. How come she had to go and tell? Now everybody's embarrassed, including me. Finally, Gretchen's new friend, who's wearing the red blouse again, says, "Y'know, my uncle had this heart attack. He was in the hospital for three months."

"My grandpa had one," says this skinny girl, "and he died."

He died! Well, that's not going to happen to my dad.

Gretchen looks up. "Jorie's dad isn't old like your grandpa. He's lots younger, and he's always been very healthy, hasn't he, Jorie?"

I feel better. "Yeah. He's always playing tennis and stuff like that."

"What's it like, Jorie?" somebody says. "I mean, what happened when he had the heart attack?"

I shrug. "I dunno. He was at the hospital when it happened."

The skinny girl swallows a bite of cake. "Have you seen him? Did they let you come and see him?"

"Yeah. He looks really awful. All white and—well, you know—really awful." I take this bite out of my apple.

"I was in the hospital once," says the girl in the

red blouse. "I had my appendix out, and boy, did it hurt after the anesthetic wore off!"

"Yeah. I had this friend who——" "My brother broke his collarbone and——" Everybody starts talking at once, and I'm sitting there eating my apple, and for some goofy reason I'm not feeling so terrible after all. Maybe Gretchen had the right idea. I guess it's not so bad when you talk about it.

After school, Mr. Stern stops me on my way out of the room. "Jorie, is something the matter with your dad?"

"Um—yes, Mr. Stern."

"My wife and I wondered. He takes care of my baby girl, y'know."

"He does? Honestly?"

"Uh huh. My wife called the office yesterday, and they said he'd be gone for a while. I hope it's not serious."

"Oh, no, it's not serious. It's really not, Mr. Stern. He—he had a heart attack, that's all."

"Oh." There's this long pause. Mr. Stern shuffles papers on his desk. "I'm sorry, Jorie. My wife thinks he's really special. And, Jorie, I'm sorry I made you move up in front. I didn't know about your dad."

"That's all right, Mr. Stern."

"Now you just take it easy. If you can't get all your homework done the first few days, it's all right. Don't worry about it. Okay?"

"Okay. Thanks, Mr. Stern."

Stephanie and I go to the first meeting of the junior high club at the community house that evening. Naturally, Craig Tanner is there playing the big-shot athlete, swinging around on his crutches and getting everybody to sign his cast. Everybody but me. I stay away from him till it's time to leave, and I find Stephanie in this group with Craig in it.

"There's a stop sign at Fifth and Elm," she's telling him

"Sure there is," says Craig, "but I didn't think——"

"Y'mean you went through a stop sign on your bike? No wonder you got hit. That was a dumb thing to do."

"C'mon, Steph. What makes you think you're so smart?"

"She's a whole lot smarter than you, Craig Tanner."

Hey, that's me talking. I wasn't going to speak to him.

He turns and grins at me. "Well, look who's getting friendly."

"Whadya mean friendly?"

"At least you're speaking to me." All of a sudden, he turns serious. "Hey, how come you didn't tell us about your dad? I'm really sorry about him. Honestly."

"Well—l, thanks."

"Hey, how about autographing my cast? After it comes off, I'm gonna keep it forever." He sways back and forth on his crutches. He makes me nervous. "Hey, you oughta draw something on there. Make a picture. You're good at that kinda thing."

Me? Draw something for posterity on Craig's cast? Is he crazy or something? He's standing there acting like some big wounded football player, giving me this dumb smile.

Well, I guess it's not so dumb. It's kind of a nice smile, actually. It's all over his face. I'm kind of flattered he asked me to draw something. I like to do stuff like that. I'm always doodling. Drawing goofy faces on my school papers. I even did the cover for our grade school literary magazine last year. It was this silly picture of a horse wearing a hat with flowers on it and glasses way down on its nose, and people seemed to like it. So now I

grab Craig's pen and draw this cartoon of myself
with hardly any nose, big eyes, and this enormous
mouth that cuts across my face.

"Looks just like you," says Craig, "with that big
mouth."

"All right, Craig Tanner, you just quit making
nasty remarks."

"Hey, I didn't mean anything."

"Sure you didn't. Come on, Steph, let's get outa
here."

On the way home Stephanie says, "He was only
kidding. How come you're so touchy? You never
used to be that way."

"Well, I am now. Craig Tanner makes me want
to puke."

On Sunday, when Mrs. Finch drives to the airport to pick up Marcia, I go along with her. She's
wearing this elegant, white-knitted jacket that
probably came from her last trip to the Bahamas.
Maybe I ought to feel sorry for her, with her
blond hair that's cut short and straight and her
red fingernails and her turned-up nose. Mom told
me once that she lost her only child, this little boy,
when he was two. He got some horrible disease,
and Dad couldn't save him, and finally he had to
tell Dr. and Mrs. Finch their boy was dead. Dad

could hardly talk for days after that.

Maybe that's why Mrs. Finch spends so much money. She's sort of a spendaholic. A long time ago, Dr. Finch got in trouble with the hospital for putting some man in the hospital who they said didn't need to be there, and collecting money for taking care of him. Only there was nothing wrong with him. Marcia and I overheard Dad and Mom talking about it, and they found out we were listening and told us not to discuss the matter with anybody. Dad and Mom thought he did it on account of Mrs. Finch's bills. They asked the Finches to dinner and made us eat early so there'd be just the four of them. Dad told us later that Dr. Finch said he was never going to do a thing like that again, and Mom said Mrs. Finch was going to quit spending all that money and not to say a word about it.

Seems as if Mrs. Finch still spends an awful lot of money, though.

When Marcia gets off the plane, the first thing she says to me is, "How's Dad?"

"I dunno. Mom looks pretty worried, Mar."

We look hard at each other, and then we look away.

"All I could do was think about him," she says,

swallowing. "I kept thinking and thinking."

"How's Gran?"

"Okay. Only she's really worried about Dad. She knows it's serious."

"Oh, Mar, you didn't tell her he's——"

"I didn't tell her he's in Cardiac Care, but what was she supposed to think when she called the hospital and couldn't talk to him? She was really mad. Her own son. Then she realized it must be bad."

"Ooh boy! I hope he gets well soon. Anyway, he's gotta be okay when she comes for Thanksgiving and Christmas. He's just gotta."

"I'm glad she's coming," says Mrs. Finch. "She's a dear old lady."

Old lady? Well, maybe Gran is kind of old, but she doesn't seem that way, and Mrs. Finch doesn't have to make a big point of it.

It isn't till we're home, with Marcia's suitcase sitting in the front hall, that I get to ask my question. I ask it while I'm hanging up Marcia's coat, as if I really don't care one way or the other. "Hey, Mar, do you happen to remember a guy named Peter who had the same adviser you did last year?"

"Who?"

"C'mon, Mar, you must remember him. He's dark and skinny."

"Well, how am I supposed to remember that long ago? Help me with my suitcase, will you?"

I grab a piece of the handle, and we bump upstairs. "He's not bad looking," I say. "He's got gorgeous brown eyes and——"

"Jorie, what's going on? How come you're telling me all about this Peter Diaz?"

"Funny that you remembered his last name all of a sudden. You even pronounced it right. You do remember him."

"Well—I, sort of."

"See, he's been working for Mr. Kirby. We had this long conversation. He's kind of touchy, but he's nice. He remembers you."

By this time we're in her room. We drop the suitcase, and I take a look at her. Her face is pink. She's blushing. She turns and plunks herself onto her big bed, on the spread with the blue forget-me-nots all over it. "How'd you know he remembers me?"

"He asked about you."

She raises her eyebrows. "Well, he did talk to me a couple of times. Asked me a couple of questions."

"But you didn't encourage him, right?"

She shrugs.

"Scared, huh?"

All of a sudden she sits up straight. "Jorie, will you please stay out of my business? I can take care of myself."

"Hey, you don't have to get all upset. I just thought you and I could wander out into the yard tomorrow afternoon. See, he comes on Mondays, and if——"

"C'mon, Jorie, that's a dumb idea. Why should I do a goofy thing like that? I don't even remember what he looks like."

"You do too."

"Will you drop the subject? Just drop it. I don't wanna talk about it."

Jorie Jenkins, the matchmaker. Big deal!

5 • Everything's Going to Change

Dr. Finch blames Dad's problems mostly on that extra weight he's been carrying around. Seems every time he tries to get up and walk, he gets these chest pains, so they have to keep him in bed a pretty long time. I've got this feeling he's going to be in Cardiac Care forever. But finally, the middle of September, Dr. Finch puts him into a regular room in the same section with other heart patients and a NO VISITORS sign on the door. All of a sudden, that room blossoms with mums and roses and lots of other flowers I never heard of.

Dad's still awfully floppy, but he's getting up and walking around, and he looks like a human being again. "Hi, sweetheart," he says to me. "You look like some cute, redheaded angel. I must be in Heaven."

His voice is shaky, but at least the words sound like Dad. At least I know he's not some wax dummy. He's going to be okay for sure. He's going to be fun again, and he'll be able to patch me up when I need it. Funny. I haven't had anything that needs fixing lately. Seemed as if Dad was always checking me out, but since he got in the hospital I haven't needed any of that. I wonder how come.

"Can I get you something, Dad? Maybe I could bring you one of your medical magazines sometime."

"No, thanks. I don't feel like reading about myself yet." He's frowning. He hardly ever used to frown.

Dr. Finch walks in. "Hello, Jorie. You behaving yourself, Charlie?"

"Can't do anything else. They don't even feed me here. I'm starving. How am I ever supposed to get to try that treadmill at the end of the hall?"

"You will, Charlie, you will."

"Listen, I've got to get back to the office. All the

work's getting shoved off on Bill Moy."

"Charlie, will you cut that out? Bill can do the work, so quit worrying."

"Okay, but——"

"No buts, Charlie. I said quit worrying. Just concentrate on losing weight and doing your exercise. That'll get you back to the office."

Dad doesn't answer. He looks sleepy. His eyelids are saggy, and his face is like oatmeal. He looks like somebody I don't know. I lean forward. "Need anything, Dad?"

"Uh uh. Just leave me alone, will you?"

Leave me alone, he said. He doesn't want me around. Hey, what's going on? What's happened with me and my dad? All of a sudden the room goes blurry.

Dr. Finch presses the button that moves Dad's bed down flat. "I'll have a look at him, Jorie. Want to go down the hall for a few minutes? He'll be all right till your mom gets back."

Out in the hall I get this vague impression of people in white coats whizzing around inside some big bubble. The treadmill at the end of the hall is all blurry. I feel this tear trickling down my cheek, and I reach for it with my tongue.

Somebody puts an arm around my shoulders.

It's Dr. Moy, Dad's partner. "Hey, Jorie, what's the problem?"

"My dad just kicked me out. He doesn't want me around."

Dr. Moy lets go of me, and the corners of his mouth turn up the tiniest bit, and his black eyes are squinting as if maybe they're smiling too. "Just because he kicked you out doesn't mean he's not still crazy about you, Jorie. If you can't be nasty to someone you care about when you feel rotten, you're in real trouble."

So Dad still feels rotten. So I guess I ought to be flattered that he feels close enough to me to pick on me. Or something like that.

I wipe my nose with the back of my hand. "Yeah. I see what you mean, I guess. But, Dr. Moy, is—is he okay? I mean, he's going to get over being like that, isn't he?"

"He's okay, Jorie. Dr. Finch tells me he's encouraged." He stops in the middle of the hall, with people going up and down it, and just stands there with that black lock of hair of his flopped over his eye and his shoulders sloping down. He isn't smiling now. He turns and gives me this long look through his big glasses with the black rims. "Look, Jorie, he's going to need to be careful for a long time, probably for the rest of his life."

The rest of his life. Holy Sam!

"So you have to watch out for him all the time. You have to take care of him without making a big thing out of it. Try not to worry him, and don't ask him to solve your problems for you. Can you manage that?"

So everything's going to change. I'm going to have to put on my own bandages, and if I get into a jam I'm going to have to work things out for myself instead of asking Dad what to do. Dad won't be Dad any more. He'll be kind of a stranger. It's scary.

Dr. Moy's black eyes are blinking at me. I nod very slowly. "Sure, Dr. Moy I can manage that."

I didn't say I was going to like it.

6 • Put 'Er There, Pardner

A couple of weeks later, Stephanie says, "Let's go watch the tryouts tonight for the junior-senior show."

"Nah. Mr. Spinner'll kick us out."

"No, he won't. We'll sit way in the back of the auditorium, and he won't even know we're there. Don't be chicken, Jorie."

"I'm not chicken." Actually, I do want to go. Besides, Stephanie's a good person to go with because she's always getting away with stuff because she's got this very innocent way of talking to grown-ups when they ask embarrassing questions. "All right, I'll go. Marcia can drive us."

The whole front of the community house auditorium is jammed with kids who are juniors and seniors in high school. There are twice as many girls as boys. Where do all the boys go at a time like this? Mr. and Mrs. Spinner are there, and after a while Mr. Spinner's on the stage pushing his glasses up his nose. "All right," he says in his enormous voice. "Quiet, everybody. Quiet. Most of you know that the junior-senior show was started sixteen years ago and is now a tradition in this town. This year's performances will be November 11 and 12. It's a variety show, with different scenes that have no connection with each other. For instance, there's one about Shirley Temple that has a tap dance in it. And a comedy scene about the First Family in the White House. Some of you may be in several scenes. All this year's scenes were written by students and passed on by the adult committee. The name of the show is *Put 'Er There, Pardner.* Nice friendly name, huh?"

Everybody giggles.

Mr. Spinner smiles. He looks like one of those round faces teachers draw on your homework when they like it. "Everybody can be part of the show. People who play an instrument can be in the orchestra. You can work with tickets, costumes, props, or scenery. So if you don't get in the show, don't worry. We have a job for you."

When I'm old enough to be in the show I'm not going to take one of those crummy jobs. I'm going to be the lead. Sometimes, I think about myself being Eliza Doolittle in *My Fair Lady* and going to the ball in an elegant, low-necked gown.

"All right now," Mr. Spinner is saying, "everyone on the side of the aisle on your right will go into the basement room and try out for singing with our musical director." He nods toward this bushy-haired man standing by the door on our right. "The rest of you will stay here and read scenes for me and Mrs. Spinner. Then you'll switch."

Everybody starts getting up and talking "Quiet, everybody," yells Mr. Spinner. "Before we start, is there anyone here who can play the piano for the singing tryouts? Just today, till we can find a regular piano player for the show?"

So Mrs. Spinner wasn't able to find anyone. I'll bet she tried everybody she could think of, but half the mothers have gone to work, and it must be harder and harder to find anybody to do stuff with us kids. There's this big silence. Nobody raises a hand. Finally, Stephanie leans forward and raises hers. "I'll do it," she calls out.

Mr. Spinner lowers his head so he can see her over the tops of his glasses. He gives her this big smile. "All right—um——"

"Stephanie. Stephanie Schmidt."

He looks puzzled. "Were you here last year, Stephanie?"

She's so tall for her age everybody thinks she's in high school. She gets up and walks down the aisle giggling and shaking her head. "I'm in seventh grade, Mr. Spinner."

"No kidding! And you really can play the piano?"

"Sure."

He points to the bushy-haired man. "Okay, Stephanie, follow that man."

Marcia's one of the ones that are left in the auditorium for the acting tryouts. "Now," says Mr. Spinner, wiping the top of his head with his handkerchief, "we're going to do parts of the last scene, the long Western scene. In this scene Miss Beulabelle, the snooty schoolteacher, is kidnapped by Big Bad Bar and his men and held for ransom because of her wealthy rancher father. After lots of action and songs, Miss Beulabelle gets rescued by Husky Harold, the cowboy who's pure and clean. Before the curtains open on this scene, Miss Beulabelle sings a solo in front of the curtains, *I'm the Belle of the Ball.* "

I can hardly wait till I'm a junior in high school. If I were in this show, I'd be Miss Beulabelle for sure. I wouldn't fool around with being in the chorus. I could sing that solo so the people in the last row could hear every word. I mean, everybody's always told me I've got the loudest voice in my class.

"Now," says Mr. Spinner, looking through the tops of his glasses, "Petunia, the barmaid, is in the scene because the action takes place in Big Bad Bar's bar. And there are all the other citizens who come in to cheer Husky Harold after he rescues Miss Beulabelle, who has been humbled by her experience and falls in love with Husky Harold. At the end, everyone sings *Put 'Er There, Pardner.* Okay, let's get some of you people in the front row onto the stage. Two boys and two girls."

Naturally, Marcia's in the last row, so it'll be hours before she gets her chance. I get out my science book and open it to the chapter on life in the desert. There are all these pictures of snakes and mice and lizards and stuff. Yuck! Mr. Stern's got this lizard in one of the tanks in our room at school that keeps staring at me. Mike O'Neil says it wants to be friends, but who wants to be friends with a lizard? Actually, the horrible truth is that slippery animals scare the socks off me. It doesn't make any sense, but there it is.

So I'm really glad when Marcia finally gets up on the stage with her friend, Amy Goodhart, and a couple of guys. They've all got scripts in their hands. Mr. and Mrs. Spinner are sitting in the front row taking notes. One guy is supposed to be Husky Harold, and the other is Big Bad Bar, and then they switch. The girls read Miss Beulabelle's lines, and Petunia the barmaid's. Marcia's doing Petunia's part first. "How come you're sneakin' down here into the saloon, Miss Beulabelle?" she says in this voice I can hardly hear. Then she says something about one of Big Bad Bar's evil men who's supposed to be guarding Miss Beulabelle, I think. Only I'm not sure. How come she doesn't talk louder? She's got to talk louder.

"Big Bad Bar's evil gang man is asleep," says Amy in this nice loud voice. "I'm surprised you can't hear him snorin' all the way down here. It's disgustin'."

Big Bad Bar makes his entrance, and then Husky Harold. They get into a fight and pull their guns, and the girls tell them to please, please quit fighting, and then, just when it's getting exciting, Mr. Spinner says, "All right, cut. Now trade parts, please."

Marcia does better with the part of Miss Beulabelle, but still I can hardly hear her. It's a shame because she's pretty and dimply, and she could be just right for the part. The way she sticks her nose in the air when she says, "It's disgustin'," would be really neat if I could hear the words.

When Marcia's leaving for the singing tryouts, Mrs. Spinner reaches out her tubby arm and stops her. They talk for a minute, and Marcia looks kind of disappointed. Wonder what's going on.

On the way home, I ask Marcia what Mrs. Spinner was talking about. Marcia looks disgusted. "She wanted to know if I'd be costume chairman. She said she wanted me to do it if I decide not to be in the show. But I know what she meant. I'm not getting a decent part after that tryout. I messed it all up. Mom probably told her I make my own clothes, and she just asked me to make me feel better, I know."

"C'mon, Marcia," says Stephanie. "You did great in your singing tryout. Honestly."

"Thanks. But Amy did a whole lot better. She takes voice lessons, y'know. Anyway, I won't get a speaking part, for sure."

"When will you find out?" says Stephanie.

"Call-backs are tomorrow at dinner time. Mr. Spinner phones you by seven if he wants you to come back for another tryout."

Marcia and I had planned to go to the hospital around five-thirty the next day, the way we usually do, to see Dad while Mom ate dinner, but Marcia decides not to go. She doesn't say so, but I know she's hoping for a call. She doesn't talk much during dinner. Guess she's still waiting.

She doesn't get the call. It's after seven.

"Anyway, you're sure to get in the chorus," I say, chewing on a piece of canned pineapple. "You did okay in the singing."

"I s'pose." She looks all droopy. Wish Mom were here. She'd know what to say. Funny. I'm missing Mom a lot lately.

"Were you scared when you tried out?"

"Sure. Everybody's scared, I suppose."

"Yeah, I suppose. Well, you don't have to be in the chorus if you don't want to, y'know. Being costume chairman may not be all that glamorous, but it's a pretty important job."

Come to think of it, it is important. Guess I never thought about costumes having to be made. Guess I thought they appeared out of thin air.

Marcia doesn't say anything. She just shrugs.

"You'd be good at it, Mar." She would, too. She makes these gorgeous clothes for herself in shades of blue and green, and she always looks clean and neat. I don't know how she does it. And the more I think about it, the more important that job seems. What kind of a show would it be without costumes? I mean, if Miss Beulabelle did that solo in jeans instead of a beautiful dress with a full skirt, the audience might not even care if she gets kidnapped.

Marcia and I show up at the hospital the next day. Dad's sitting in a chair waiting for his dinner. "Guess what, Dad," I say. "They want Mar to be costume chairman for the junior-senior show."

He turns his head and squints at Marcia. "Hey, how about that?"

"Do you think I should do it, Dad? It's a lot of work. It'd be a whole lot harder than being in the chorus."

Dad wrinkles his eyebrows as if he's trying to think, but he just can't seem to. All of a sudden, I remember what Dr. Moy said about not bugging him. "Listen, Mar, it's your life, isn't it? You gotta make up your own mind, so quit bugging Dad."

She raises her eyebrows in this surprised way.

"For heaven's sake, Jorie, what's the matter with you? Dad always used to give me advice."

"So now he's busy getting himself well."

"Anyway, how am I supposed to decide?"

"Easy. Do what you feel like doing."

"I don't know what I feel like doing."

"Well, if you don't know, who does?"

She shrugs. She screws up her face and stares at the floor. "Okay, I'll do what I feel like doing. I'll do costumes."

Dad gives her this teeny smile, and she sits up straight in her chair. Guess she feels better now that she's made up her mind. I'm glad she's going to do costumes. They're about the most important part of the show.

7 • What's Embarrassing About a Furnace?

That crazy lizard is staring again. It sits up there in its glass cage behind Mr. Stern and blinks at me from behind his left elbow all during science class. I can hardly concentrate on listening to Mike O'Neil's paper on the ecology of the desert. How come I've got to be in the front seat? I've got nobody to hide behind.

Mike lays his paper down on my desk and turns and actually takes that slithery lizard out of its cage. "Lizards can be up to twelve feet long," he says, holding it up. "But, as you see, this one is only about six inches. It's a type of lizard called an American chameleon. It's got four very short legs, and it's got these eyelids, and holes for ears. Its skin can change color so it can hide on stones and stuff. It's scaly." He runs his hand down its body, all the way to its tail, while I shudder.

All of a sudden, the lizard wiggles loose. It falls onto my desk, scattering Mike's papers all around, slipping and sliding into my lap. Holy Sam, it's trying to climb up my front! "Get it out of here. Go away, you—you——Hey, somebody, get it out of here!" I stand up and try to knock it off of my blouse, but it hangs on tight. It looks just as scared as I am.

Mike yanks it off, but it slips out of his hand onto the floor and starts to crawl up my leg. It feels like wet noodles with sand in them. Ugh!

Half the kids are yelling, and the other half are gathered around me trying to do something. Mr. Stern is trying to get to me, but he can't get through. "Just stand still, Jorie. Stand still, will you?"

Fat chance. I'm stamping my foot all over the aisle, trying to shake that lizard. Half the kids are trying to grab my leg. Once I accidentally kick Craig's crutch, and he almost falls over. Serves him right.

Mr. Stern finally gets to me. "Hold still, Jorie." He puts his hands on my arms. "Will you hold still for a minute? Take it easy now. It's okay. Just take it easy."

For some reason I hold still.

Mike reaches down and grabs the lizard and holds it tightly up against his chest. He pets it and pets it, and it doesn't wiggle the tiniest bit. It just keeps staring at me. It must be mad at me.

I feel pretty stupid. The kids are looking at me as if I'm some kind of nut, especially Craig.

"Try petting it," says Mike. "Just reach over and put your finger on its head and pet it. Go on, Jorie."

Everybody's watching. Craig's got this disgusted look on his face. Well, I'll show him. I reach out and touch the lizard's head, and it blinks at me. I run my finger down its body. "See?" says Mike, "it's not all that bad." Even Craig is nodding.

But I don't think I'll ever get used to lizards. They aren't my thing. They can go their way, and I'll go mine. I mean, they're just too slippery. And besides, they don't have any personality.

After science class, on the way to English, Gretchen catches up to me. "Y'know, Jorie, I think that lizard likes you. Did you ever notice it keeps looking at you?"

"Yeah, I noticed. I wish it would cut that out.

I feel pretty silly, but I just can't stand icky things like that."

"You're not silly. You just gotta get used to stuff like that. I'll bet you're more used to it than you were before."

"Yeah. But I'm kind of ashamed of myself. I made an awful lot of fuss over a six-inch lizard."

She giggles. "Well, everybody's got something to feel silly about. With me it's the dentist. I can't stand to go to the dentist."

"No kidding!"

"No kidding. I get so shivery I think I'm gonna die."

I never talked to Gretchen like this. All through grade school I thought she was really stupid, but she's got a certain amount of sense after all.

I feel pretty dumb in English class too. Mrs. Gordon hands me back my poem. It's called *Frustration*, and it's about Sparks and the way he's been feeling lately. She gave me a C. "This isn't a bad poem, Jorie," she wrote at the bottom of the page, "but you're capable of doing much better. For instance, your use of the simile 'like a sail without wind' is trite. You can think of something better to describe an unhappy dog."

Well, I don't think a sail without wind is the tiniest bit trite, and that's exactly what Sparks reminds me of. But I guess this just isn't my day. Everything's going wrong.

Things get better during the last period, in my elective art class. We're working with acrylics, and Mr. Chipworth wants us to do a portrait. I paint this clown in the rain, holding a teeny umbrella over his fat red nose. How come I always do funny pictures, even when I'm feeling rotten? When Mr. Chipworth squints through his horn-rimmed glasses at my picture, he says, "That's excellent, Jorie. Those cheeks could be a little less bright so they don't take away from the nose. But I like it."

"Thanks, Mr. Chipworth."

"Bring it back on Monday when I change the pictures in the glass case in the hall. I want to put it up."

"Sure, Mr. Chipworth, I'll do that."

It turns out that's the one nice thing that happens to me all day.

When I get home that afternoon I check out Mom's vegetable garden. It's after Halloween, and there are weeds all over the place, so the garden looks like some South American jungle.

But there are still a couple of squashes on the vines, and I pick them for dinner. All of a sudden, this voice says, "Hi."

It's Peter. He's leaning on the fence between our yard and Mr. Kirby's. He looks even taller than the last time I saw him.

"Hi. You still around?"

"Yeah. I came over specially, to rake leaves and check out Mr. Kirby's furnace for winter."

"Whadya mean check out his furnace?"

"Didn't you know? You gotta have it checked for gas leaks and stuff sometime in the fall. You don't want it to explode or anything. I suppose your mom takes care of getting somebody to do yours."

"Yeah. Only she probably hasn't done it this year. See, she spends all her time at the hospital with Dad."

"How come?"

"Didn't I tell you? My dad had this heart attack."

He lets his breath out slowly. "Hey, that's terrible. How—how is he?"

"Not so good. They keep putting him back in Cardiac Care. He can't seem to lose enough weight, and now he's got this thing called phlebitis. Blood clots in both legs." I sigh. "I wonder if he's ever gonna make that treadmill."

"Huh?"

"Oh, never mind."

"Wish I'd known about him. I would've—well, I would've done something. Listen, what can I do? I'll check your furnace for you."

"Okay. I wouldn't want it to explode."

"I'll come over as soon as I finish here."

He's hoping he'll see Marcia. But she's got a costume committee meeting, and anyway I don't think she'd hardly speak to him. "Just come in the back door and through the kitchen," I say. All of a sudden, I remember what I wanted to ask him. "Hey, how did you get out of Cuba?"

He gives me this long look, as if he's trying to decide whether or not to answer me. "We flew."

"Y'mean you just got in a plane and took off?"

He nods. "My mom and my uncle and I. See, this was a long time ago, when I was three. The government was letting people do that if they had plane fare."

"Where was your dad?"

He looks down at the fence and gives it a kick. "He was dead. They killed him. The government killed him. He had his own business, and he and the government didn't get along."

"Ooh boy! I'm sorry, Peter. Honest."

"That's okay. It was a long time ago."

"You must've been rich."

He ignores me. "See, Dad told Mom if anything like that ever happened, she and I should get out of the country. So we flew to Miami with my uncle. We had to leave everything behind, and Mom didn't want my uncle to have to worry about us, so we came here as soon as we could."

"Wowie! That trip to Miami must've been scary."

"Yeah. We weren't sure they were actually letting us go. A month later they wouldn't have."

I yank the stem out of a squash and chew on it. "What's your mom doing?"

"She works at the library."

I must have seen her there. There's this blond woman at the main desk who couldn't possibly be Peter's mother, and there's this dark woman with wavy hair and a smile that makes you feel special. "Hey, is that your mom at the main desk? The one with wavy hair?"

"Yeah."

"I've seen her lots of times." I certainly never suspected she escaped from Cuba a month before they quit letting people out.

"You go to the library a lot?" says Peter.

"Nah. Not as much as Mar. Mar reads a lot."

"Hey, does she? So do I. See, I got this new car ——Well, it's not exactly new. It's secondhand, and I fixed it up. Anyway, I drive over there almost every day after I finish here or at the supermarket, and I read engineering and mechanics magazines before I take Mom home when the library closes at six."

"Y'mean you go over there every single afternoon?"

"Sure. Every day but Sunday and Wednesday. Mom doesn't work those days."

Wonder how come he never saw Marcia there. Probably because he doesn't get there till after five. He must read a lot of those magazines if he can fix furnaces and cars and all that stuff. He must be smart.

I'm upstairs doing math homework when I hear Peter come in and clump down the basement stairs. A couple of minutes later the door of my room bursts open. It's Marcia. "Jorie, for heaven's sake! How come you asked that—that Peter into our house?"

"C'mon, Mar. I didn't even know you were home."

"Well, I am. We called off the meeting to work

on our costumes. I was down in the basement pressing seams with these rollers in my hair looking absolutely awful, and down he comes. Ooh, Jorie, I could kill you!"

Now I notice she's got rollers in her hair. But she always looks okay, even with her hair up. She's got this costume over her arm that's almost finished, all pink and white and ruffly. It's for Amy Goodhart, who's going to be Miss Beulabelle.

"Hey, I'm sorry. See, you gotta get your furnace checked every fall so it doesn't explode, and——"

"I know. He explained that to me. It was so embarrassing."

"Whadya mean embarrassing? What's embarrassing about a furnace?"

"I don't mean that. I mean the rollers. I'm getting ready for the French Club dinner tonight, and——Honestly, Jorie, you might've checked before you sent him down there."

Poor Peter! He's never going to get to know Marcia. She must like him or she wouldn't be so upset about a few dumb rollers. So if she likes him, how come she's mad when she gets a chance to know him? She doesn't make any sense.

8 • How Can You Be Scared of Somebody You Like?

Marcia's going to that French Club thing at the high school means she won't be going to the hospital, and I'm going to have to get my own dinner. Boy-oh-boy, do I miss Mom's cooking! Marcia's been doing it lately, and a lot of it is experimental, like the chicken casserole she spilled curry powder in. Makes me feel like some guinea pig. And I've got to walk Sparks all the time and do dishes and shop on Saturdays, and I'm always forgetting the really important stuff like eggs or laundry soap or caramel topping.

Around five, I grab the picture I did in painting class and leave for the hospital. Maybe the picture will cheer Dad up. He's back in a regular room for about the millionth time, but he still hasn't got started on that treadmill.

The hospital's only four blocks away, but it's taking forever because I'm dragging myself along Chestnut Avenue. I feel droopy. I mean, how could anything else go wrong? On top of all the other stuff, I'm probably not eating enough vegetables, and I know Sparks isn't eating right either, and our house is all sloppy except after Mom's cleaning lady comes on Thursdays, and I'm not doing fun things with Stephanie any more. She's playing for rehearsals in the evenings because Mrs. Spinner never did find another piano player, and she has to do homework in the afternoons. I don't even have any reason to cut out doing homework the way Mr. Stern said I could.

All of a sudden, there's this honk and screech of tires. Holy Sam! I almost got run over. I stepped right out in front of a car. Here I am on High Street, with all the hospital traffic on it, and I didn't even realize. I stare at the driver, who's shaking his head, and I just keep walking.

At the hospital the woman at the front desk smiles at me, and I give her this sick smile back. At the nursing station in the section where the heart patients are, somebody says, "Hi, Jorie."

"Hi." I don't even look. I go right on into Dad's room. Mom's in a chair knitting, and Dad's in his special phlebitis chair that keeps his legs propped up. His legs look better, and I think he's finally losing some more weight.

"Hello, sweetheart." He looks gloomy. What happened to that big smile he used to give me? Is he ever going to get it back?

Mom puts down her knitting and gets up. Seems as if she's the one who's really getting skinny. "How did Mrs. Gordon like your poem?" she says.

I shrug. "Okay, I guess." I don't want to talk about my poem.

"Something the matter, Jorie?"

"Nah. I just feel blah, that's all."

She gets this worried look on her face.

After she goes to dinner, Dad says, "How's my girl friend Stephanie?"

That's more like it. He always used to call Stephanie his girl friend, but he hasn't even mentioned her for a long time.

"She's fine. She's playing the piano for the junior-senior show rehearsals, y'know, so she's really busy."

MARCELLUS LIBRARY
Marcellus Community Schools

He's not listening. He's wearing that tiny frown again, the one that makes him look as if something's bothering him, and he can't figure out what it is. When you talk to him he doesn't answer most of the time. He just gets that frown.

I'm aching to tell him lots of other things. Like about the lizard, and about my poem, and about how Marcia likes Peter but won't even let him get near her. I want to ask him how you can be scared of somebody you like. But on account of the frown, and on account of what Dr. Moy said, I bite my lip.

I don't know what to say. I don't know how to behave with Dad any more. I'm afraid I'll say something wrong, or do something wrong. That's another thing that's bugging me. In fact, it's got to be the thing that's bugging me most of all, now that I think of it.

"Mar's at the French Club dinner," I say. It ought to be okay to say that.

"French dinner, huh? Say, I wish your mom and I could have gone this year. Those kids really cooked up a meal for us parents last year, with all kinds of fantastic food I couldn't pronounce."

"Yeah. And you got this call right in the middle of the lemon soufflé and had to rush to the emergency room."

He nods. "Did I ever hate leaving that dinner! I even remembered some of my French from high school. *S'il vous plaît, mademoiselle.*" He gives this little chuckle.

Sometimes, it's almost like old times with him.

Maybe this is the time to show him my clown picture. I dig it out of my jacket pocket and hold it up.

He blinks at it. "Hey, that's—that's nice, Jorie. Nice colors."

His eyes are halfway closed. He doesn't really care. He looks tired. He's almost frowning.

Sometimes it's like old times, but most of the time it isn't.

After a while, I go down to the nursing station and tell the nurse in charge of Dad's room that he wants a shave in the morning. Out of the corner of my eye I see Mom across the hall, passing the little lounge next to the elevators, coming back from her dinner. She's smiling. She looks happier than she has since—well, since Dad had his heart attack. "Jorie, I just met Dave Finch in the hall. He says Dad's ready to start on the treadmill and will probably be home in about a week. Isn't that terrific? That means he'll be there way before Gran comes."

"Hey, that's—that's great." I'm glad. I really am glad. But still, I feel shaky.

Mom gives me this funny look. "What's wrong, Jorie? Aren't you glad?"

"Oh, sure. Honestly, I don't know what's wrong. I'm glad, only——"

"Only what, honey?"

"Only I never know what to say to him any more. He's not the same, Mom. He's different. He —he even scares me the tiniest bit."

I wish I hadn't said that. She's got enough problems without listening to me blubber about the way I feel. Anyway, I probably shouldn't feel that way. It's not right. She's going to think there's something wrong with me. She'll think I'm being stupid. But she doesn't seem to. She takes hold of my elbow and sits me down next to her on the sofa in the lounge. "He is different, isn't he? It bothers me too, Jorie."

So she feels the same. My mom feels the way I do. Well, why shouldn't she? How come I'm surprised? "There's nothing we can do about it, is there, Mom?"

She shakes her head. "We can't change him back to being the way he was. You have to remember it's toughest of all on him. His whole life has changed, honey. You know he feels rotten a lot of the time. And besides, he has to get used to not being able to take care of the whole world. He has to quit letting that get him down. There are a lot of new things we're all going to have to learn to live with."

"Yeah. Hey, Mom, how can you be scared of somebody you like?"

She puts her hand on my arm. "You're only scared when there's something about the person you don't understand. We have to get to know the new things about Dad."

Funny. That's the second time today I've wondered about being scared of somebody you like. "And Marcia has to get to know about Peter," I say.

"Peter?"

"He's the Cuban boy that likes Marcia." All of a sudden I find myself telling her about Peter, and about how Marcia's scared of him, and about how dumb I feel about that lizard business, and about Craig's calling me a big mouth, and about missing Mom's cooking and being sick of doing dishes and taking Sparks out all the time, and about not being able to do things with Stephanie, and about how Mrs. Gordon didn't like that sail business in my poem. It all comes out like one big, enormous upchuck, and I feel a whole lot better. Only Mom won't understand that all this stuff is important, even though maybe it doesn't seem that way. Anyway, I shouldn't have bothered her with it. It wasn't fair.

"I shouldn't have said all that, Mom. You've got enough to worry about."

"But I'm glad you did. It's important."

It's important, she said.

"Jorie, I've been worried about you. You've been acting as if you're made of stone, and that's not good for you. I was afraid you were sick."

"Well, I do feel kind of icky sometimes."

"I know. We all do, honey."

I give her this very intense look. She's got shadows under her eyes and caves where her cheeks used to be. "You feel okay, Mom?"

She looks down and plays with her watch. "You know, Dave Finch thinks I ought to get away sometimes to rest and do other things, now that Dad's better. He says Dad should mostly take care of himself. He can certainly take his evening exercise without me. So maybe I could take over Stephanie's job playing the piano so she can spend more time with other things. I don't think

Dad would mind if I'm gone in the evenings for rehearsals. I love doing it, and I know it would do me a lot of good, and Dad has friends all around him here. I could even start tonight."

"Hey, that's great. The show's only a week off, and it's taking lots of Steph's time. She's getting behind in her work, and she needs time to get ready for her fall recital tomorrow, and for just goofing around. And, Mom, I could come here sometimes in the evenings if you thought Dad needed somebody. I mean, with Marcia busy with costumes and all."

Mom smiles. "You're growing up, Jorie. You know, I think he might like that once in a while. You could get to know each other better and not be so scared of each other."

Scared of each other? Is Dad scared of me the way I'm scared of him? I never thought about that.

9 • Marcia and Peter

If you get to know things about somebody, you're not scared of that person any more. That's what Mom said. So how can Marcia get to know things about Peter?

There's this cast party after the Saturday night performance of the junior-senior show, and you can bring a date if you want to. I'm positive she'd like to ask Peter. But she won't, of course. Not unless she's just about forced into it.

So maybe if I tell her about how he and his mom escaped from Cuba, she'll get over being scared. I'm not exactly sure if that's what Mom meant, but at least I can try. Then I can watch for my chance to get them together somehow. I mean, he likes to read and she likes to read, so all

I have to do is think of some way to get her to the library the same time he's there. Sure, it's meddling in other people's business, but this is an emergency.

The junior high club is going to the Friday night performance and then having refreshments in the community house basement. That's opening night. Mom's the tiniest bit worried about Dad because she'll be playing the piano with the orchestra, and I'll be watching the show with the club, and Marcia'll be backstage helping people change from innocent little girls in the Shirley Temple scene into wicked barmaids with hearts of gold in the Western scene. But Dr. Finch says not to worry, that Dad's got friends all around him, and that he's getting used to not having somebody there in the evenings to take out his dinner tray when the nurse's aid gets busy somewhere else, and that he can't see any reason why they should have to get in touch with us.

Mom gets home pretty late from rehearsals. "Last night it was the Shirley Temple scene," she says at breakfast on Saturday. "The tap dance is really tricky. And there's a special rehearsal this afternoon for the White House scene. Well, maybe I can dash over and see Dad this morning after I pay the bills. I haven't paid them for over two months, and I'm afraid the power company will turn off our electricity."

"Don't worry about this afternoon, Mom. Steph and I'll drop in after her recital."

She smiles. For some reason she looks awfully little. "Thanks, honey. I can go this evening. The Finches asked me to dinner, but I don't want to go." She stirs her coffee slowly. She knocks the spoon against the side of the mug to get rid of the drip, lays the spoon on the table, and gives this enormous sigh. "Sometimes I get sick of going places alone."

Funny. She never said anything like that before. She's gone out by herself lots of times, when Dad got stuck at the hospital, or else got some call when they're all dressed and ready to leave for somewhere, and he says he'll meet her there, and sometimes he does and sometimes he doesn't.

Do I want to marry a doctor? Well, I'd have to love him an awful lot if I did. Come to think of it, Mom must love Dad an awful lot.

Stephanie's dad and mom drive us to the recital at the piano teacher's house. Stephanie's third from last on my typed program, which means she's one of the best players. The little kids are first, the girls in their frilly dresses and the boys in their clean shirts and big ears. They play stuff like *Pixie Waltz* and *The Happy Farmer,* and it's really boring. I can hardly keep from twitching, and if I weren't sitting between Stephanie's parents I think I'd get up and go out for a walk. After a while, it starts to get more interesting, especially when some fat guy who can hardly reach the pedals plays this Hungarian dance. It comes to me that he was once a fat little beginner. These kids have got to learn somehow, so I try to be tolerant.

Finally, it's Stephanie's turn. She gets up there looking gorgeous in this new lavender dress her mom got for her and zings into her Chopin waltz as if she's been doing it ten times a day, which she probably has. Mr. Schmidt, next to me, sits up straight. She makes only this one teeny mistake, and when she's through everybody claps like mad, and Mrs. Schmidt loses her cool and wipes her eyes the way my own mom did after I acted the Chinese daughter in the sixth grade play.

After it's all over, we have soft drinks and cookies while everybody gushes over Stephanie. Later, in the car, I say, "You were terrific, Steph."

"Thanks." She's still the tiniest bit pink from the excitement.

"Hey, Mr. Schmidt, would you mind dropping me off at the hospital? I'm gonna go see Dad. Wanna come, Steph? You know he's crazy about you."

"Nah. I'd really like to, honestly, but I've got to get home and—um—help Mom with dinner. She's having company."

She doesn't want to see Dad. She always used to think he was terrific, but I think she's scared to go. Well, maybe I don't blame her.

At the hospital, Dad's lying in bed breathing hard. I inch into the room and say "Dad" a couple of times, but he doesn't even wiggle. Just goes on breathing deeply. He's asleep. Actually I'm relieved. It's awful when you can't talk to somebody because you're not supposed to upset him, or else because he won't listen. I ought to do what Mom said. I ought to try to get to know him again, but I don't know how. I say "Dad" once more, but not very loud. Nothing happens, so I hurry out of the room and down the hall sort of as if I'm running away, which maybe I am.

Dr. Finch is down at the nursing station writing out some notes. "Hello, Carrots."

"Hello, Dr. Finch." I'm going to tell him. I've got to. "Dr. Finch, there's something I've got to tell you. See—well, maybe it doesn't seem very important, but I can't stand getting called Carrots. I really do hate it, Dr. Finch."

He looks up. He's got gloom lines all over his face. "I didn't know. I'm sorry—um—Jorie. I'm glad you told me."

"Thanks a lot." I give him this big smile, but he doesn't smile back. How come? He makes me feel funny. "Say, Mom's sorry she can't come to your dinner party tonight. She's awfully tired all the time, and——"

"There's not going to be any dinner party."

"No party? Is—is Mrs. Finch sick or something?"

"I wouldn't know," he says in this sort of cracked voice, as if maybe he's going to cry. "I moved out day before yesterday. You might as well know, Jorie. We're separated."

Separated! No wonder he's so gloomy. "Hey, I—I'm sorry, Dr. Finch. Honestly." I would go and bring up that Carrots business at a time like this.

He swallows hard. For some reason, I feel awfully bad for him. All of a sudden, he seems human. Even his mustache looks human. It's not quite even, and it's drooping. I guess even Dr. Finch can feel bad sometimes. I suppose Mrs.

Finch just couldn't stop spending money, and I guess he couldn't stop her from doing it. So all this time he's been taking care of Dad he's been having problems of his own.

"Don't be sorry, Jorie. It was something that had to happen. It's better now that we've decided to separate."

Why is he telling me this? It makes me feel squirmy. I start backing away. I want to get out of here fast. "I guess you're right, Dr. Finch. I'm sorry I brought up that Carrots business. It wasn't exactly the time for——I mean——Well, I've got to run." I turn and hurry down the hall.

How come I keep running away from people? Funny. I can't see how come Marcia's afraid of Peter, and here I am, afraid of Dr. Finch and afraid of my own dad, and I'm acting crazy.

Anyway, I'm not afraid of Marcia. I'm going to tell her about Peter.

The next afternoon, Sunday afternoon, I'm in her room sitting on the bed while she sews fake roses the color of wine onto Miss Beulabelle's hat. "So he and his mom and his uncle just barely got out of Cuba. I mean, they were the last ones out. Well, almost, anyway. When they got to Miami, they were all just about half dead, and then his mom had to work terribly hard to make enough money to get them here."

Marcia's leaning over so far I can't tell what her reaction is to my story. Finally, she looks up. There's this misty look in her eyes. She's got to be impressed. Well, I did my best. "That's really something," she says. "That really is something all right. Did he tell you that?"

"Sure. How else would I find out?"

"He didn't exactly hold back on the scary details, did he? Think he was trying to impress you?"

She can be an awful pain. She really can.

"Oh, Mar, for heaven's sake! I kept throwing questions at him. What was he supposed to say?"

"Well—l, I dunno."

I stretch out on the bedspread, all over the blue forget-me-nots, trying to act nonchalant. "Hey— um—you busy after school tomorrow?"

"Maybe. I've got to call Amy and see if she can come over for a fitting. We've done everybody but her, and the costume's finished except for the lace trim on one of the ruffles. My sewing machine's busted, so I've got to do that by hand."

"Can't you do the fitting some other time? See, there's this library book I've got to get for my book report on Tuesday, and I need you to drive me there."

"Jorie, what's got into you? You never asked me to drive you before. You always walked or took the bus."

"I know. But if I do that there won't be time to go see Dad. We ought to do that, y'know."

"Oh, all right. Maybe I can do the fitting at rehearsal tomorrow night." She nods toward her desk, where she's got about a dozen books piled up. "Anyway, I've got to return all those costume books to the art department. They were due last week, and I haven't had time to get them back."

The next day, I time it so we get to the library around five-twenty. I had to go to an awful lot of trouble stalling her off so we'd get there about the same time as Peter. I hid one of her books, and she was really frantic because those books are special. I mean, they're full of these gorgeous costume illustrations. They've got to be really expensive. I found it in her closet at just the right minute, and when she said, "How in the world did it get there?" I just gave this innocent shrug.

Right after we pull into the library parking lot, this beat-up, little red car comes roaring in and parks a few places from us. It's Peter. Just as we're passing the back of his car with our arms full of Marcia's books, he dashes out from between his car and the next one and crashes into Marcia so she dumps her books all over the pavement. Ooh boy!

Peter stands there with his mouth open. "Marcia! Hey, I'm sorry. Hey, I really am sorry. I didn't mean——"

"Did you have to go and barge into me?" She's almost in tears. All those expensive books are every which way, with one of them open, face down, so the pages are bent.

Peter's on his knees, picking up the books and putting them in a pile. "I'll carry 'em in for you. Listen, if there's any charge for this one, I'll pay it. See, I was in this big hurry to get the November *Mechanics Today*. It's supposed to come out today with this article on gasoline substitutes."

"Know anything about sewing machines?" I say. "Marcia's is busted."

"Hey, maybe I could fix it."

"Don't bother," says Marcia. "It's fine. It's really fine."

I could kill her.

"Hey, these books are beautiful," says Peter, as if he actually doesn't care about the sewing machine. "You interested in costumes?"

She's just standing there giving him this icy stare, while he talks and talks. I'm beginning to feel sorry for him. "Marcia's costume chairman for the junior-senior show at the community house this Friday and Saturday," I say very distinctly.

"No kidding! Hey, could I come see it?"

"It's sold out." Marcia's still just standing there watching him, while I think of all the nasty things I'm going to say to her later.

Seems as if every time I plan something I just make things worse. She's being so obnoxious I can't see why Peter still seems to like her. I should think he'd hate her.

But when I come out of the library stacks with *Pride and Prejudice* and meet them coming out of the art department, she's saying, "That was nice of you to pay for the messy pages. I've got to admit that was really nice."

I'll bet paying for those messy pages took a big chunk out of what he earned from Mr. Kirby this afternoon. Maybe all of it. Thank goodness Marcia at least has enough sense to appreciate it.

At the front desk, Mrs. Diaz checks out my book. Peter introduces us to her, and she gives us her special smile. Then she gets serious. "Peter has told me about your father. He's better?" She's got this really gorgeous accent.

"Oh, yes," says Marcia. "He's better. He's probably coming home Sunday or Monday."

"That's very nice," she says. "Peter was worried."

On the way out to the car with Marcia, I say, "I'll bet Peter would love to come to the cast party. He doesn't have to go to the show to do that."

"Well, I'm not going to ask him, if that's what you mean."

"You scared to ask him?"

Her face goes pink. " 'Course not. I just don't want to, that's all. What would we talk about?"

"Hundreds of things. How about gasoline substitutes? Say, maybe you could find out how we could run the car on the weeds from Mom's garden."

"Oh, Jorie!"

She's scared if she asked him he might say no. She's acting crazy too. We both are.

10 • I Can Do It

Marcia says the dress rehearsal on Thursday night was awful. In the White House scene the wall collapsed on the President and his wife. Shirley Temple forgot to bring her wig. When Big Bad Bar went to pull the gun out of his holster to shoot Husky Harold, there wasn't any gun. And the mayor kept forgetting his lines.

Mom sets oatmeal on the breakfast table. "I guess there never was a dress rehearsal that went right. It's always this way. Remember last year, Marcia?"

"Yeah. But last year I wasn't responsible for any wig. That dummy wanted to practice at home with it on, and I told her to be sure and bring it back. How come she didn't do it?"

"She'll bring it tonight," says Mom. "She's no dummy. She'll want to look right for her parents, or her boyfriend."

The show starts at eight-thirty, and Stephanie and I are meeting the junior high club at the community house at eight-fifteen. Mom and Marcia have to be there early, so I'm the one who stops in at the hospital after dinner to check on Dad. He's due to come home on Monday, so this should be almost the last time I need to visit him. Stephanie and her dad are going to pick me up at the hospital.

When I get to Dad's floor I'm just in time to see Dr. Finch, in his white coat, disappear into Dad's room. In the room there's this nurse, and a resident who's giving Dad a shot. Dr. Finch leans over Dad.

Dad's eyes are half closed. "Now listen, Dave," he says in this sleepy voice, "you're not going to put me back upstairs."

"Just temporarily, Charlie. Just to keep a check on you, that's all. You'll be out of there in no time."

Dad groans.

Dr. Finch looks up. "Oh, hello, Jorie. Your dad's having a little—um—problem, that's all,

and we're taking precautions. Wait out in the
hall, will you?"

"Sure. Sure, but——"

"I'll be out in a minute. I want to talk to you."

Out in the hall, I lean against the wall. How
come he wants to talk to me? My legs feel like
squashed bananas. The minute seems like a year.
Will Dad ever get home? Will he spend the rest of
his life going up and down like some bouncing
ball?

Finally, Dr. Finch comes out. "Your mom
around?"

"Uh uh. She's got to play for the junior-senior
show tonight, but if it's an emergency——"

"It's not an emergency. It's only that your dad
had some chest pain again. He almost fell while
he was on the treadmill. The resident got him
back to the room, but his heart has some rhythm
disturbance, so the nurse called me. These
things happen sometimes. I guess you know
that, Jorie. Anyway, the problem's usually not
serious."

It's usually not serious, he said. I shut my eyes.
My whole life flashes in front of me. My whole
life with Dad, anyway. I picture him smiling and
laughing and putting his big, comfortable arm

around me. I picture him the way he used to be, the way I remember him.

I open my eyes. "Maybe I'd better stick around. Would that help?"

"Sure. Come on up to Cardiac Care. Keep him company, Jorie. I've never seen him so discouraged. Talk to him. Let him know you're around."

Up in Cardiac Care, I can hardly remember how come I was mad at Dad after he got sick. All that business seems pretty stupid now. I stand next to his bed. "Hi, Dad."

He opens his eyes. "Jorie."

"You feel okay?"

"I feel rotten. And I feel so—so weak. I hate that. I hate feeling weak."

"I know. But you'd better get used to it. Everybody feels weak sometimes, so how come you're so special?"

He gives me this long look. "I've got to admit you've got sense, Jorie."

"Right. Hey, Dad, you'll be okay if you give yourself time."

"But it's been so long."

"I know, Dad."

I feel awfully close to him. I wish I could talk

about the way I feel, but your heart can't talk, and I guess it doesn't need to.

He gives me this little smile. "So how come you're hanging onto my hand so tight my bones are about to break?"

Ooh boy! I didn't realize. I let go of his hand, and we both start to laugh. It's a different kind of laugh from when we used to laugh together. It's more grown-up.

He closes his eyes, and finally he goes off to sleep.

All of a sudden I remember. Stephanie and her dad are picking me up at five after eight. It must be nearly time. I tell the nurse I'll be right back and zoom out of the room. The clock over the elevator says exactly five after. Downstairs, Mr. Schmidt is just pulling the car up to the main door. "Steph, I can't go. Dad's got this—um—problem. It's not serious, but I'm staying with him."

Mr. Schmidt gets this worried look. "Anything we can do, Jorie?"

"Nope. Just don't tell Mom or Marcia. It would spoil the show for 'em."

"You're brave, Jorie," says Stephanie. "You really are. Hey, what about your ticket?"

What about my ticket? Somebody ought to be able to use it. All of a sudden I think of Peter. I yank the ticket out of my wallet and stick it under Stephanie's nose. "Turn this in at the ticket table, will you? Tell 'em it's for Peter Diaz."

"Peter Diaz?"

"D-I-A-Z. Got it?"

"Got it."

Back in the hospital the clock says eight minutes after eight. I hunt up a phone and look up Diaz on Seventeenth Street. "Peter?"

"Yeah."

"It's Jorie. Listen, you wanted to go to the junior-senior show?"

"Yeah."

"Can you be at the community house in twenty minutes?"

"Y'mean right now? But I was going to——"

"Marcia's backstage working with costumes."

"Well—um—sure. Sure I can go."

"Okay. There's this extra ticket. I haven't got time to explain. It's at the ticket table. It's in your name, and you can pick it up."

"Okay. Thanks, Jorie."

Back in Cardiac Care, the nurse tells me I can wait in the little room down the hall where they have magazines and stuff. Funny. I don't mind so much being around Dad now. Maybe it's because I was there when he was feeling really rotten, to hold his hand, even though I did almost break his bones. For some crazy reason I feel as if I know him better than ever before. Maybe because I understand the tiniest bit how he feels. It's a different feeling from the way I felt before, but it's a lot closer.

It seems like hours that I stay there, all by myself, reading some magazine all full of articles on how to decorate your house and how to entertain in a three-room apartment. Every once in a while I check to see if Dad's awake, and the nurse lets me go in and put my hand on his shoulder, just to show him I'm there. Back in the waiting room, I almost fall asleep, but I make myself stay awake. I want to be sure Dad's okay.

Finally, just when I feel I really am going to fall asleep, Mom walks in. "Jorie, are you all right? Stephanie told me about Dad after the show."

"I'm fine, Mom."

"The nurse says he's all right now. He should be back downstairs soon. She said you were terrific, honey, that you stayed around all the time. She thinks that made a lot of difference. And I know it wasn't easy for you."

"Yes, it was, Mom. It wasn't hard at all."

11 • Thanksgiving

It's like some kind of miracle when Marcia and Peter actually do get together. He comes backstage after the show on Friday night and asks her out for pizza, and by the time he brings her home she knows a whole lot about gasoline substitutes, and he knows about American costumes, and he's going to come on Sunday to fix her sewing machine. So she figures the least she can do is to ask him to the cast party. Wish I'd been around when she did that. It must have been something.

But I have to settle for her telling me about it later because I'm busy somewhere else. See, when Mom comes to the hospital after the show to get me, she insists on driving me to the community house for the junior high club after-the-show refreshments. "You missed the show, honey, but there's no reason you shouldn't have a little fun tonight. You deserve it."

At the soft drink table, Stephanie and Craig and a bunch of others come up and tell me I was some kind of heroine for staying with Dad. I don't feel like any heroine.

Craig sticks around with this serious look on his face. "Your dad okay, Jorie?"

"Yeah. He's a whole lot better. But I hope he can make it home for Thanksgiving. See, Gran's coming. She comes every year for Thanksgiving and stays for Christmas, and——" Hey, how come my eyes are getting blurry so I can hardly see Craig? How come my cheeks are all wet? This is awful. Craig's going to laugh at me for sure.

He doesn't laugh at me. He hands me this big, messy white blob. "Here," he says. "Wanna blow?"

I grab the handkerchief and blow. What's the matter with me? The crisis is over, and now I'm crying. I can't talk. My voice might crack. I wander off into this dark corner away from the stereo, and Craig follows me. Maybe so he can keep track of his messy handkerchief. After a while, I quit blubbering. I'm only sniffling.

"You okay?" says Craig.

"Yeah. I don't know what's the matter with me. I must be tired or relieved or something."

"Anyway, I'm glad your dad's better. Remember when he and your mom chaperoned the sixth grade picnic? He was fun. And, Jorie, I'm sorry I made that crack about your big mouth. You've been going through a lot lately, and—well, I guess I just didn't think."

"Well, thanks for the handkerchief. I'll take it home and wash it for you."

"Aw, never mind. Just keep it. It's left over from when I had a cold last winter."

Anyway, he didn't follow me just to get his handkerchief back. Maybe he even likes me the tiniest bit. Maybe that's why he picked on me.

I stuff the handkerchief in my pocket. "I'm sorry I kicked your crutch that day in class. It was nothing personal." All of a sudden, I realize he hasn't got his crutches, and his cast has disappeared. "Hey, what happened to your cast?"

"Had it taken off yesterday. I wondered when you'd notice. I might even be able to go out for basketball if my foot keeps getting better." He's smiling that smile of his that spreads all over his face. For some goofy reason it makes me feel a whole lot better.

He and I sit in that corner together for ages. He

tells me about how you make a basket from the left side in basketball, and about how he's going to do his science project on monkeys. I'm glad monkeys aren't slithery. I tell him I'm going to do my project on pigments and oils, because paints are made out of stuff like that. I ask him how the show went tonight, and he says somebody kept turning left in the tap dance when she should have turned right, but the costumes were gorgeous and Amy did a terrific job in the Western scene. "Wish you'd been with us, Jorie." He smiles again.

Hey, maybe I wish I'd been there too.

On Saturday night I do get to the show, though. Mom talked to Mrs. Spinner and explained what happened, and Mrs. Spinner said I could have special permission to stand at the back of the auditorium with Marcia and the rest of the committee people during the action.

Right there in the program it says, "Costume Chairman . . . Marcia Jenkins." Hey, that's neat. And during the show my feet don't even feel the least bit tired. The wall stays up during the White House scene, Shirley Temple is wearing her wig, and everybody turns the right way in the tap dance. In the last scene, the Western scene, Big

Bad Bar has a gun in his holster, and the mayor remembers his lines. But the big hit of the show is Amy, in that pink and white dress and her shiny black hair and the hat with wine-colored roses that Marcia made for her. She looks so elegant everybody gasps when she comes out in front of the curtains. Then she sings in that terrific voice of hers, so we can hear every word.

I'm the belle of the ball, the pick of the crop,
The top of the heap, the best in the shop.
I'm the peach without blemish, the quality choice.
I'll lasso every man within sound of my voice.

Hurray, hurray for me!
I'm as gorgeous as can be.

All you envious gals, try and top me, just try.
All the cowboys love Beula, and b'gosh, so do I!

Everybody claps and cheers, and Big Bad Bar's evil men, who've come out to kidnap her, have to duck backstage again while she takes about a million bows.

All the kids in the show are in that last scene. When it's over, after Miss Beulabelle has gotten humble, and after she's gone into a clinch with

Husky Harold, and after everybody's sung "Put 'er there, pardner, put 'er there," the parents and sisters and brothers and boyfriends and girl friends in the audience stand up and clap and cheer, and Amy bursts into tears right up there on the stage.

Afterward, backstage, Amy rushes up to Marcia and throws her arms around her and says it would have been nothing without Marcia and wipes her nose on the sleeve of her costume because there's no place else, and Marcia's smiling so hard she's got these deep, deep dimples.

The whole thing is absolutely sensational.

Well, I don't have to worry about Marcia any more. I only have to worry about Dad.

A few days later he gets back on the treadmill. He exercises a little bit more each day. He doesn't get any more chest pains or anything, and finally, on Monday, Dr. Finch says he's doing so well he can come home Wednesday afternoon, the day before Thanksgiving. He's got to be extremely careful, though. Dr. Finch gives special orders for him to take everything slowly, not to lift anything heavy, and not to take any calls from patients. Dr. Moy will go on handling all the calls for two or three more weeks. After that Dad will get back into practicing very slowly, but Dr. Moy will do most of the night and weekend work. Meanwhile, they're trying to get a younger doctor into the office.

So Dad's home a few hours before Gran arrives. I mean, he's actually home, looking lots thinner, and he's actually sitting in the big chair in the den in a T-shirt and an old pair of slacks three sizes too big watching some absolutely crucial football game on TV. We left him there with Sparks all around him, rubbing his ear against Dad's leg, licking his tennis shoes, all frisky, like—yeah— like a sail that finally got some wind.

Marcia and Peter are out picking up Gran at the 7:50 plane from Tucson. They went off in Peter's car, jabbering to each other as if they were trying to make up for lost time. Mom's in the kitchen making cranberry sauce for tomorrow, and I'm in the living room doodling spaceships on the back of a magazine and listening to Stephanie play ragtime, when the phone rings. I rush into the den and answer. It's some woman. "May I speak with Dr. Jenkins, please?"

"He can't come to the phone. May I take a message?"

"Is this his daughter?"

"Uh huh. I'm Jorie."

"Well, Jorie, you see I work at the hospital gift shop with your mother, and I really must speak to your dad. I heard he was coming home, and my daughter Delia has a fever."

"I'm sorry about your daughter Delia, but Dad can't come to the phone. Doctor's orders. Try calling Dr. Moy."

"Dr. Moy? But I don't trust Dr. Moy."

"I can't see why not. My dad trusts him."

"Jorie, I really must insist on speaking to your father."

"You can insist all you like, but I can't let you."

"Well, of all the rude——" She hangs up.

"Who was that?" says Dad.

"Somebody who has a daughter named Delia."

"I could've talked to her."

"You wouldn't have wanted to. She's a battle-ax. She would've chopped you up in little pieces."

He laughs. "All right, sweetheart. Thanks for rescuing me."

Thank goodness I can make him laugh. Since that evening in the hospital we're hardly scared of each other any more. Anyway, Dad's never going to get back to the office if he talks to upset parents, especially parents who don't trust Japanese-American doctors.

I wander out in the kitchen. "Can I help, Mom?"

"Sure. You can stir the sauce while I polish spoons. Don't cook it too long. Just till everything gets mixed together and the cranberries are slightly mushy."

I make sure to shove the handle of the saucepan over the stove before I turn on the heat. At least I've learned that much since September.

When the front doorbell rings I say, "I'll get it, Mom." The cranberries are slightly mushy, and I remember to turn off the heat, but I can't resist snitching a quick taste of the sauce. It's boiling hot, but it's good.

Craig's at the door holding this package wrapped in foil. "Hi, Jorie. You've got cranberry sauce on your nose. You oughta save it for the turkey tomorrow."

"Very funny, Craig Tanner. C'mon in and lemme see what you've got."

"It's my special cinnamon rolls. I made 'em to celebrate your dad's coming home, and you can have 'em for breakfast tomorrow. See, you make biscuit dough and roll it out and spread cinnamon and sugar and melted butter on it, and then you roll it up and slice it."

"Hey, that's terrific. I didn't know you could cook."

"I can't. These are the only things I can make, but they're quality stuff." He limps down the hall and into the den and dumps them on the table next to Dad. "Welcome home, Dr. Jenkins. Remember me from the time you chaperoned the sixth grade picnic?"

"Sure, Craig. You were the captain of the team that beat my team in baseball. Jorie, would you turn off the TV? My team just lost again."

When we hear Marcia and Peter drive up with Gran, Dad gets up and starts down the hall toward the front door, but Craig beats him there. "I'll help Peter with the luggage, Dr. Jenkins."

Craig's getting awfully polite all of a sudden.

Dad's frowning. He's got to be upset that he can't tear out to meet Gran and help with her luggage. Always before he used to rush up to her in the airport waiting room and grab her in his arms and give her this enormous hug. When her suitcases got coughed up by the conveyor belt thing, he'd swing them down as if they were full of cotton, even though one of them is always crammed with Christmas presents.

Now there's nothing for me to say. I'm not

going to give him a bunch of baloney about how easy it's going to be for him to let other people do things, so I just go up to him and snuggle against his arm. He reaches over and puts his finger up to my nose. "Hey," he says in his teasing voice, "you've got cranberry sauce on your nose." I'm kind of glad I forgot to wash it off. He hasn't pushed my nose for ages.

Gran rushes in with Peter and Marcia. She always seems to be in this big hurry to see us. Mom dashes out of the kitchen and kisses her, and then Dad gets his chance. "Well, Charlie," she says, tipping her head back the way she always has to do when she looks at him, "you've lost a few pounds, thank heaven. You look tired, but you look all right. I was scared silly." Gran always gets right to the point. She doesn't fool around. "Isn't it amazing the way you've snapped back? Look at you, Charlie. It's going to be like old times."

"Sure. Just like old times," says Dad. Then he adds under his breath, "Almost."

Mom puts her arm around him, and he musses her hair. Am I jealous? Well, not the way I used to be. After all, Dad could never ever make it without Mom.

Gran flashes a smile at Stephanie, and one at Craig, and finally she spots me. "Good heavens, Jorie, you look so—so grown up. I like the way you look, honey. You've changed."

I give her this big hug. "Oh, c'mon, Gran. I haven't changed the least bit."

Or have I?

MARCELLUS LIBRARY
Marcellus Community Schools

FIC
BAT

Bates, Betty

The ups and downs of
Jorie Jenkins

DATE			

MARCELLUS LIBRARY
Marcellus Community Schools

© THE BAKER & TAYLOR CO.